Focus Sound & More

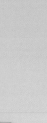L & **Simple Phrases**

I like...
I love...

Teach the Sound

TYPICAL AGE RANGE

Development: 3-6.5
Mastery: 5-7

HOW TO SAY THE /l/ SOUND

* Have child lift & place her tongue tip right behind upper teeth (diagram #1), then say the /l/ sound.
* If child struggles with tongue placement (diagram #1), have child stick her tongue out and softly bite down (diagram #2), then say the /l/ sound.

TIP ("Jelly Spot")

Using a tongue depressor, place a little jelly right behind the upper teeth and refer to this spot as the "jelly spot". Ask child to touch the "jelly spot" with her tongue tip to say the proper /l/ sound.

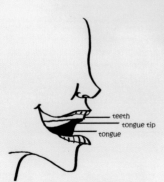

teeth
tongue tip
tongue

#1

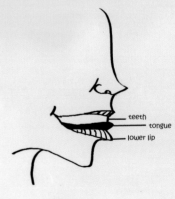

teeth
tongue
lower lip

#2

Speak With Me

ASK

Can you say, "eellllllll"?

If child struggles saying a clear /l/,
review TEACH THE SOUND.
If child says a clear /l/,
it's time to SPEAK WITH ME!

INSTRUCTIONS

1- Sit face-to-face with child to show proper modeling of the /l/ sound.
2- Start by pronouncing the beginning sound, pausing,
then pronouncing the ending sound. Have child repeat after you.
3- Slowly eliminate the pause until the sounds are said together.
4- Don't forget to **praise** a child with **encouraging phrases**
such as: "Good Try," "Great Effort," "Nice Sound!"

Picture:
Sit
Face-to-Face

BEGINNING L

l (pause) ah   (*ah* as in *all*)
l (pause) a   (*a* as in *lamp*)
l (pause) i   (*i* as in *lip*)
l (pause) o   (*o* as in *low*)
l (pause) oo   (*oo* as in *loon*)

ENDING L

ah (pause) l   (*ah* as in *all*)
a   (pause) l   (*a* as in *lamp*)
i   (pause) l   (*i* as in *lip*)
o   (pause) l   (*o* as in *low*)
oo (pause) l   (*oo* as in *loon*)

MIDDLE L

ah - l - ah   (*ah* as in *all*)
a - l - a   (*a* as in *lamp*)
i - l - i   (*i* as in *lip*)
o - l - o   (*o* as in *low*)
oo - l - oo   (*oo* as in *loon*)

PRAISE!   BE PATIENT!   HAVE FUN!

Read the Story

Step 1. TEACH a) **Sound**, b) **Word**, c) **Phrase**

Step 2. MODEL *Slowly* and *clearly* read the story out loud.

Step 3. PROMPT *Pause* and en*courage* child to repeat.

Sound
First, *say* the beginning sound, "lll". *Pause* and *encourage* child to repeat the sound.
Word
Second, *say* the end of the word, "eap". *Pause* and *encourage* child to repeat.
Third, *say* the complete word and *encourage* child to repeat after you, "lll-eap".
 If child doesn't say it on her own, have her repeat after you *(see sample dialogue).*
Phrase
Finally, *say* the simple phrase. Prompt child to repeat by asking, "What does Lovely Lily say? I love to lll...". *Pause* and *encourage* child to finish the phrase ("I love to leap around all day.").

SAMPLE DIALOGUE

Word Breakdown (leap)
The /l/ sound is said 2 times, then /eap/
The /l/ sound is said 1 time, then /eap/
Both sounds are said together, "leap."

Have child repeat every sound.

Adult: lll
Child: lll
Adult: lll (pause) eap
Child: -eap
Adult: Almost, Try Again!
Watch my mouth. llll

Lovely Lily

by Angela Holzer, MA
illustrated by Angela Hansen

Speak With Me Books is a trademark of Good Sound Publishing. www.GoodSoundPublishing.com

----

LOVELY LILY. Copyright © 2009 by Good Sound Publishing
Dedicated to all the Lily's out there! Particularly Kathryn's little girl :)...thanks lambie! You're a true friend.
Written by Angela Holzer, MA. Illustrated by Angela Hansen. All Rights Reserved. Printed in the U.S.A.
No part of this book may be reproduced or copied in any form without written permission from
the publisher unless otherwise noted on the individual page. Front cover design by Angela Hansen.
For information please address Good Sound Publishing, Palo Alto CA 94303.

Library of Congress Control Number: 2008909929
ISBN-13, 978-0-9821563-2-2 ----- ISBN-10, 0-9821563-2-4

For Information about **Speak With Me Books** or other products, please visit us at
www.SpeakWithMeBooks.com.

Good Sound Publishing™

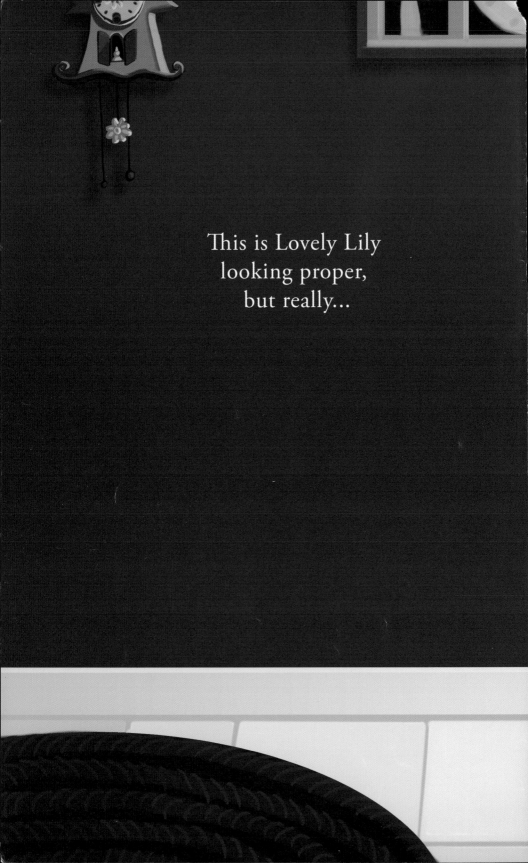

This is Lovely Lily
looking proper,
but really...

She likes to wiggle,

And sometimes giggle,

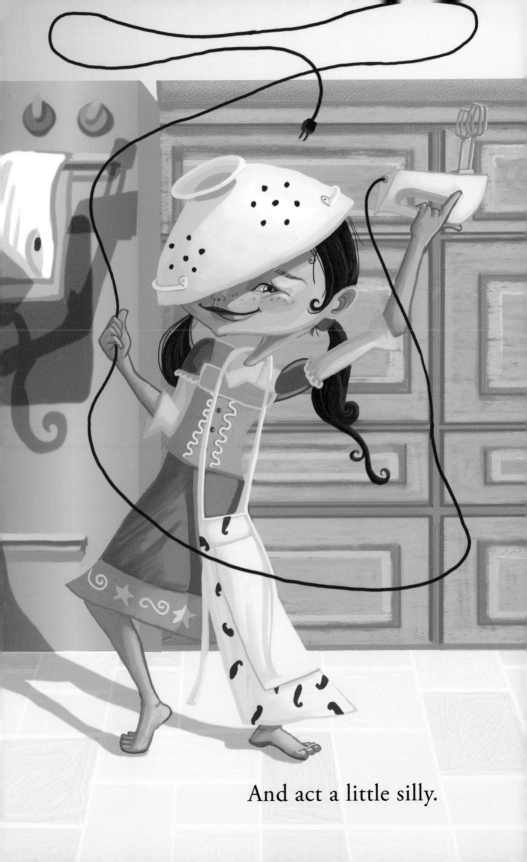

And act a little silly.

"La La La,"
Lily likes to sing!

And laugh, "Ha Ha,"
Out loud, a funny thing.

But most of all
She has a ball,

"I like,

While on her way
She likes to say,

No love,

No REALLY love...

To LEAP

around all day!"

Leap,

Leap,

LEAP,

Lily LOVES to Leap!

Leaping over lions
    Leaping over loons,

Leaping over Wizard
    Turning lizards into moons.

Leaping over leopards
Leaping over llamas,

Leaping over Ladybug
Who's wearing pink pajamas.

Leap,

Leap,

Leap,

Lily loves to LEAP!

Leaping with a lamp
Leaping with a light,
Leaping with a lasso
While flying through the night.

Poor Lovely Lily
Felt a little silly,
Landing... CRUNCH!

In Lambie's lunch

Of chips
and green chili.

Oh la la,
Lily was a mess.

She laughs, "Ha Ha,"
Because she must confess...

"Now since I'm green
I won't be seen,

Through grass or trees
Cause if you please...

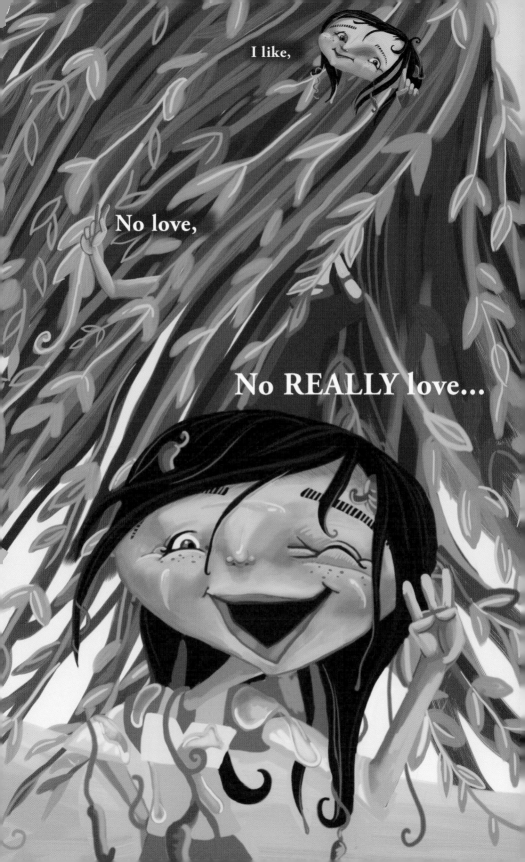

To LEAP

so no one sees!"